Christmas IN Seattle

Sue Carabine

Illustrations by
Shauna Mooney Kawasaki

GIBBS·SMITH
P
PUBLISHER

SALT LAKE CITY

04 03 02 01 00 99   6 5 4 3 2 1

Book design by Mary Ellen Thompson,
TTA Design
Printed and bound in Hong Kong

Published by
Gibbs Smith, Publisher
P.O. Box 667
Layton, Utah 84041

Orders: (1-800) 748-5439
E-mail: info@gibbs-smith.com
Website: www.gibbs-smith.com

ISBN 0-87905-929-X

'Twas the night before Christmas
up in the Northwest,
And the folks in Seattle
were feeling their best.

Some last-minute shoppers
were paying their fare
To jump on the monorail
to Pioneer Square.

Kids urging their parents, saying,
"Hurry, be quick,
Or we'll miss that great
Christmas Parade of the Ships."

We must hang our stockings,
and Nick's cookies must bake;
Please, let's get going
or he'll have none to take."

So mamas and papas,
finished up what they'd started,
And soon left behind
a forlorn Pike Place Market.

This was, after all,
a most heavenly season,
And they'd let their kids have
what they wanted—within reason!

Most people's hearts
were as light as a feather,
And not many were giving
much thought to the weather.

There had been a light rain
for most part of the day
And now snow was blowing
across Elliot Bay.

The snowflakes got bigger
as the storm spread inland,
And couples snuggled close
as they walked hand in hand.

Dads teased their youngsters
with, "Oh, dear, no!
Maybe Santa got stuck and
his reindeer won't go!"

Now as we all know,
nothing stops old St. Nick,
And the routes that he travels
are most carefully picked.

As he headed up north
and flew over Rainier,
He saw beautiful lights
of Seattle appear!

The reindeer were cruising
just as fast as they could,
Their most favorite folks lived
in this neck of the woods!

Then all of a sudden
visibility was gone,
And the number of miles
Santa saw ahead: None!

Where were the Kingdome
and Discovery Park?
He stared and he squinted,
but things were so dark.

To Dasher and Dancer
he yelled out, "Whoa!"
But before they had time
to begin to go slow

Something strange had appeared
right there in their path,
And if Nick's hands had not
been so full he might laugh.

The last thing he remembered,
he'd flown by a seagull,
And now here he was, stuck
atop the Space Needle!

He pushed and he pulled
and he twisted—no luck.
On this night before Christmas
stuck 600 feet up!

What was he to do,
there was no time to delay.
His children would suffer
if he didn't get on his way.

Well, not only was Nick
in this dire predicament
But below in the restaurant
the mayor pulled a ligament.

He was there with his family and
some of his friends
When they heard a loud crash
and were spinning on end!

The revolving restaurant
was out of control,
The chef hanging on for dear life,
the poor soul!

Well, no one was hurt,
except for their pride,
Some even confessed
they'd enjoyed the thrill ride.

Now when they'd slowed down
and reached normal pace,
Removed gravy from hairdos
and egg from their face,

They heard a loud yelling
from way up on high
Went out to the deck
and gazed up at the sky—

They couldn't believe what
had happened to Nick,
And when they thought
of the kids, well,
it just made them sick.

Something had to be done
and done right away.
They yelled back up to Nick
and had this to say:

"Don't worry, dear Santa,
we'll all go for help,
Try to stay calm, and please,
Rudolph, don't yelp.

"We'll find a way to remove
you from there;
You look so ungainly stuck
up in the air."

So the mayor of Seattle said
he would take charge,
And use KOMO News 4
to address the public at large.

Santa needed some help
from all who were around,
From Lake Washington
out toward Puget Sound.

The guys at the navy
shipyard making merry
Said they'd like to help,
as did those on the ferry.

Then the mayor, well, he heard
from Pacific Science Center,
'Cause the brilliant nerds there
said they would be mentors.

So they put forth a plan
that they knew just might work,
And the mayor, when he heard it,
felt quite a perk!

A call was then placed
to the Boeing Airport folk,
Who at first when they listened
thought it was a joke:

Santa Claus stuck with his
reindeer up high
On Seattle's Space Needle?—
they laughed till they cried!

But they got in the spirit
with all strength they could muster
And soon had adapted
two very large thrusters.

They were quickly transported
out to the Space Needle,
Then the thrusters were hoisted
to Santa, who wheedled

Them onto his sleigh
just as quick as a wink,
And he laughed and he giggled
and felt in the pink!

But, alas and alack,
that didn't quite make it—
A little more power
was needed to shake it.

So they turned to Plan B
and with paper and pen,
Listed the names of
the tall and strong men.

Now, there in Seattle
are heroes galore,
Among them are sportsmen
whom all fans adore.

The Sonics, the Seahawks,
and Mariners, too,
If they helped unstick Santa,
'twould be quite a coup!

A ladder they'd build
made of men strong and tall,
To reach up and push Santa,
sled, reindeer, and all!

The Seahawks as foundation,
the Mariners climbed next,
On the top were the Sonics;
They shoved, but were vexed.

The crowd was so sad,
and a small child who stood by
Said, "Please let me help push
St. Nick to the sky."

So he climbed to the top
and yelled, "All push on three,"
So everyone counted
as loud as could be.

Then with one final effort
to the heavens the sleigh soared,
The crowd and the athletes
and child, how they roared!

And a most thankful Santa
called back in delight,
"Merry Christmas, dear Seattle,
a most grateful Good Night!"